Dragon
for
Breakfast

Dragon for Breakfast

by Eunice and Nigel McMullen

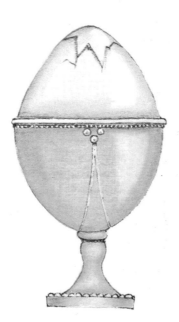

 Carolrhoda Books, Inc./Minneapolis

To Lindsey

This edition first published 1990 by Carolrhoda Books, Inc.
Originally published by Macmillan Children's Books, London.
Text and illustrations copyright © 1985 by Eunice and Nigel McMullen.
All rights to this edition reserved by Carolrhoda Books, Inc.

Library of Congress Cataloging-In-Publication Data

McMullen, Eunice.
  Dragon for breakfast / by Eunice and Nigel McMullen.
    p.   cm.
  Summary: Much to his surprise, King Ulf's breakfast egg contains
a small dragon, who grows up to be a friendly nuisance until the king
can find him a special job.
  ISBN 0-87614-650-7
  [1. Dragons—Fiction. 2. Kings, queens, rulers—Fiction.]
  I. McMullen, Nigel. II. Title.
PZ7.M4787925Dr   1990
[E]—dc20   90-36832
                                                    CIP
                                                     AC

Manufactured in the United States of America

1 2 3 4 5 6 7 8 9 10 00 99 98 97 96 95 94 93 92 91

A long time ago, in a land of mountains and lakes,
stood a fine castle...

...where there lived a king named Ulf.

Ulf was a kind king, but he could be grumpy, especially if his breakfast was late. And on this particular morning, it was very late.

To make things even worse, the top hadn't been taken off his soft-boiled egg.

Ulf gave the eggshell a sharp tap with his spoon. There was a strange squeaky noise—and then a tiny head popped out.

King Ulf couldn't believe his eyes. A little dragon with smoke coming from his nose crawled out of the shell. He wiggled his wings and began to wash himself.

King Ulf stared and stared.

He forgot that he was hungry.

He even forgot that he was grumpy.

"Fetch the queen!" he yelled to the cook.

The dragon hopped onto the king's hand. First the little creature looked at the king's mustache, then at his long royal chain. King Ulf was speechless.

When the queen arrived, followed by the royal servants, the little dragon was busy eating the king's breakfast.

Soon the dragon looked up and spoke for the first time.

"Hello," he said. "My name is Grog. I'm a dragon."

"So I see," said the king. "And you're eating my breakfast—what's left of it anyway. First you pop out of my egg, and now you're eating my toast!"

"Your Majesty," said the cook, "I'll make you a new breakfast with a real egg and fresh toast."

"Humph," said the king.

Meanwhile, the dragon was doing a handstand. The queen started to laugh, but King Ulf was not amused.

"Leave the king's presence!" he ordered the queen and the royal servants.

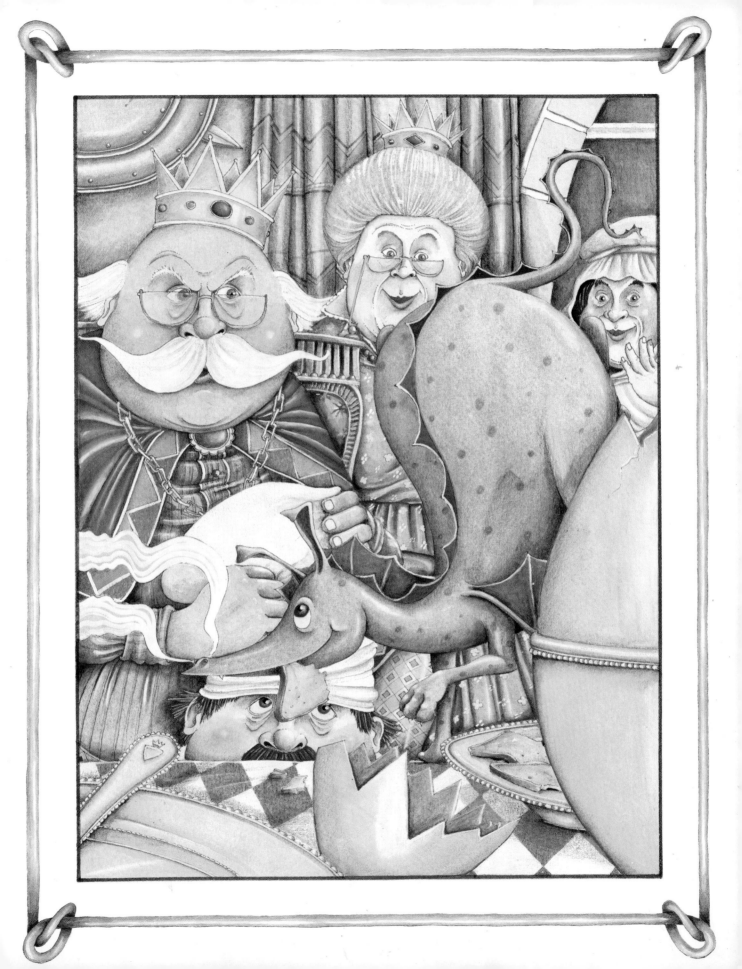

"Now, young dragon, I can't have this sort of
foolishness. If you want to stay here, you will have to
behave yourself."

"I'll try," said Grog.

"I don't want you getting under my feet," said King Ulf.
"So off you go to the kitchen! The cook will look
after you."

Grog liked his new home. There was so much
to eat! Three weeks later, he looked like a very
different dragon.

Grog thought he was very grown up, so he tried his best to help around the castle. But somehow things never seemed to go right.

He tried to light the candles—but he lit the cook's hat instead.

He did his best to help with the laundry—but he ended up setting fire to the king's socks and the queen's underwear.

He even tried to make the beds—but that was a disaster too. Then he tried to help around the kitchen, but the cook didn't like the way Grog helped. The cook got angrier and angrier, until one day he decided that Grog had helped enough.

"That's it!" he said, stamping his foot. "That dragon's got to go!"

The cook called a meeting of all the royal servants.

"Something's got to be done about that dragon," he said.

The royal laundrywoman agreed.

The royal housemaids agreed.

Everyone agreed. So they formed a committee and went to see the king.

"Your Majesty," they said, "that dragon is not a royal servant—he's a royal nuisance. Grog must go—or else we'll go on strike!"

King Ulf was horrified! There hadn't been a strike in the kingdom for a hundred years. That would mean no beds made, no fires lit, and no breakfast served.

The king sat up all night worrying. What could he do?

"I must talk to that dragon," he decided. So early the next morning, King Ulf went to look for Grog.

Grog knew he was in trouble, so he tried to hide. But the king soon found him.

"You're going to send me away, aren't you?" wept the dragon.

But King Ulf had a kind heart. "I don't know what to do. Be a good dragon and blow your nose, will you?" he said, giving Grog his handkerchief.

Grog did as he was told, and the handkerchief quickly burst into flames.

The king chuckled—he had just had a brilliant idea.

"You and all the royal servants will come to the throne room at nine o'clock," he commanded.

Later, when everyone had gathered, King Ulf cleared his throat and puffed out his chest.

"I have an important announcement to make," he said. "I've decided to give Grog a very special job."

"Well, I hope it's not in the kitchen," muttered the cook.

"I don't want his help making the beds," said a housemaid.

"All he's good for is burning things," grumbled the royal laundrywoman.

"Exactly," said the king. "From now on, Grog will be the royal firelighter. He will be the only one allowed to light the castle fires."

Everyone cheered, even the cook! Because of the king's plan, the royal servants wouldn't have to go on strike.

Grog glowed with pride as the king placed the badge of royal firelighter around his neck. He was a very happy dragon.

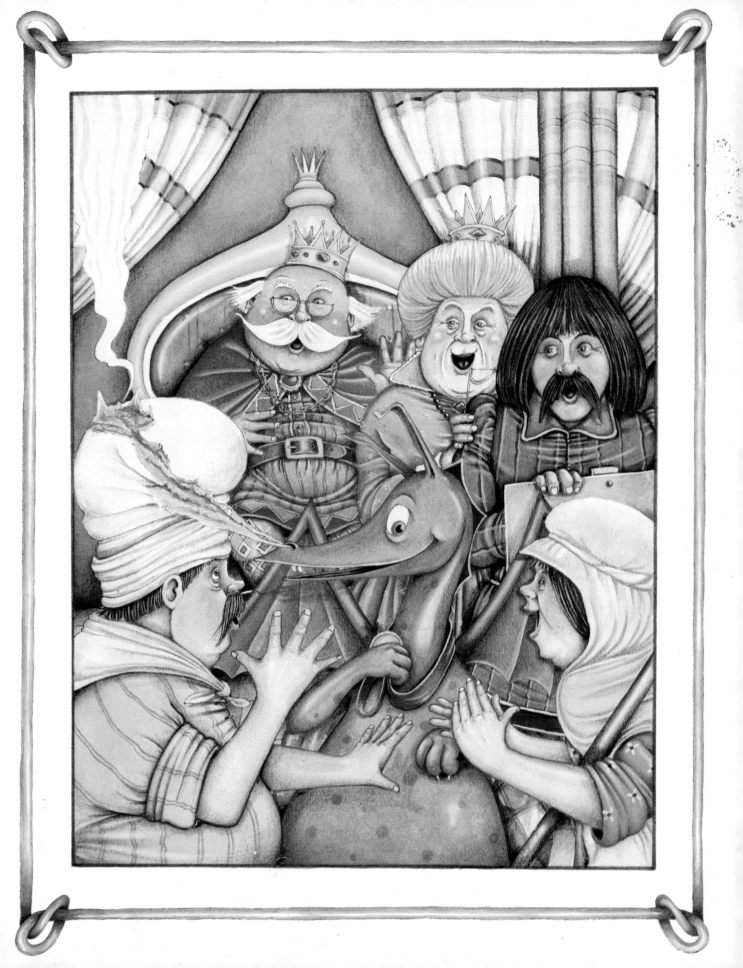

The next morning, Grog woke up early and crept downstairs to begin his new job. But first he wanted to show the king how grateful he was. He decided to make the king's breakfast and take it to him in bed. He took extra care to make sure nothing was burned. When Grog had everything ready, he tiptoed quietly along the hallway and knocked on the king's bedroom door.

A sleepy voice answered, "Come in."

Grog proudly carried the breakfast tray to the royal bed.

The king gazed in horror as the egg on the plate began to crack open by itself.

"Oh, no! Not again!" he whispered. "It couldn't happen again."

The eggshell cracked a little more.

"But there aren't enough fires in the castle for two dragons!" wailed King Ulf.

The shell gave a final crack, and out popped the tiny head of a little chick.

The king stared.

Then he chuckled.

And then he burst into roars of laughter.

Grog, the royal firelighter, just smiled.

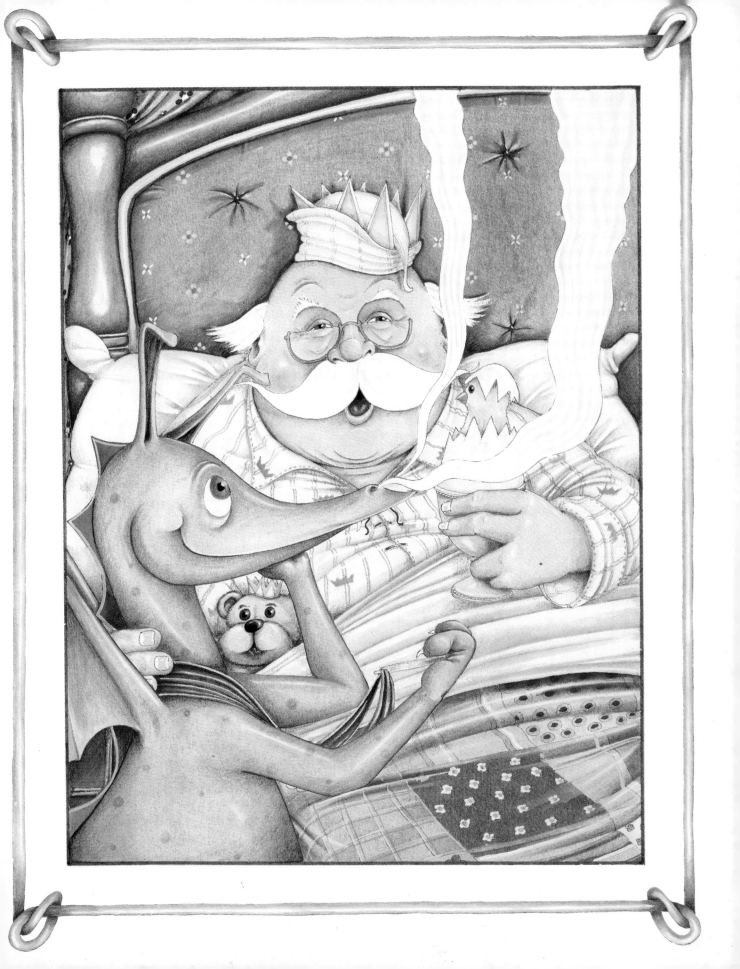

The End